SCROOGE'S
NIGHT BEFORE
CHRISTMAS

JULIE PETERSEN

ILLUSTRATED BY
SHERYL DICKERT

GIBBS SMITH
TO ENRICH AND INSPIRE HUMANKIND

'Twas the night before Christmas,
  and old Marley was dead,
As dead as a doornail,
  so the simile read.
His former partner, Scrooge,
  walked to their office,
Thinking of nothing but his own
  profits and losses.

Scrooge scolded Bob Cratchit and
   forbade him more coal,
For the heat gave no warmth
   to old Scrooge's cold soul.
Though the day was a joyful
   part of the season,
For Scrooge 'twas an annoyance,
   and here was his reason:

Christmas picked his pocket
   every 25th of December,
A loss of business was all that
   Scrooge cared to remember.
His stony heart was ice
   as it beat in his chest.
He ignored the needy, the hungry,
   and all of the rest.

No cheer could Scrooge spare,
  even for his own kin.
His nephew's festive greeting
  could not muster a grin.
"Why be merry?" Scrooge grumbled;
  his shoulders did shrug.
"A Merry Christmas, indeed!
  Bah! Humbug!"

When two gentleman came,
  imploring for charity,
Scrooge denied a contribution
  with great asperity.
"To prisons and workhouses!
  Send all the poor there!
Decrease the surplus population.
  I do not care."

Through the frost and the fog,
   Scrooge walked to his place,
When there—on his knocker—
   he saw Marley's face!
It was there! Then 'twas gone.
   Gone just as swiftly.
Scrooge hurried inside,
   his heart beating quite quickly.

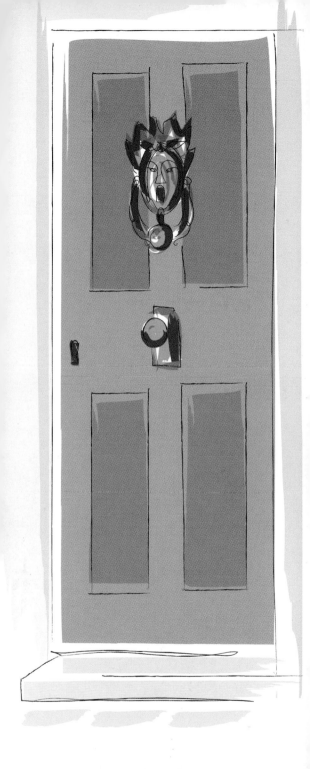

His dark, dusty rooms
were silent and plain.
Then Scrooge heard a moan
and the scrape of a chain.
Fettered and worn,
limped out Marley's pale ghost.
With a groan and a shudder
he spoke to his host.

"Scrooge, I have come
your callous soul to help save.
Behold! This fate will be yours
upon meeting your grave.
These cold, heavy chains
I had forged through my life.
Yours are longer still,
leaden with sorrow and strife.

Your rest will be haunted
   by three spirits tonight.
They're the only chance
   and hope for your plight.
Heed their counsel and change
   your uncaring heart.
As the bell tolls one,
   the first visit will start."

Marley's specter vanished
    with a cloying clang,
And fear gripped Scrooge
    as one bell clearly rang.
Filling the dark room
    shone a light bright and vast,
Emitting from the kind
    Ghost of Christmas Past.

"Come," she spoke gently,
    "rise and walk with me.
We shall look in the shadows
    of what used to be."
Back they flew
    to a previous Christmas morn,
And spied a young boy, Scrooge,
    alone and forlorn.

They watched as Christmases
passed, each one spent alone,
Without family, without friends,
without even a home.
Then as a young man,
Scrooge was in Fezziwig's employ,
And there Christmas was spent
in laughter and joy.

Old Scrooge felt a pang
   as he remembered those years
And how he now treated Bob Cratchit
   with scorn and with jeers.
The ghost and old Scrooge
   then observed from above
As he was bid farewell
   by his dear former love.

Scrooge's relish for money
   outweighed his love for her.
They could never go back
   to the way that they were.
This last scene chiseled at
   old Scrooge's chilly heart,
And he bade the First Ghost
   to finally depart.

As the bells chimed two,
    Scrooge was back in his house,
Where nothing was stirring,
    not even a mouse.
Then a light gleamed intensely
    from under the door,
And Scrooge heard a sound
    he had not heard before.

Then what to Scrooge's
 wide eyes should appear,
But a jovial ghost
 with a long, bright red beard.
"Come in! Come in!"
 pealed out a jolly bellow.
"Look upon me and know me
 better, good fellow!"

"I'm the Ghost of Christmas Present,"
laughed the genial phantom.
He took reticent Scrooge
    on a journey across the kingdom,
Where people all around reveled
    in the joy of the day,
Feasting and merrymaking,
    all in their own way.

The spirit led Scrooge to
    Bob Cratchit's poor dwelling,
Where the smell of goose dinner
    was rising and swelling.
The whole family rejoiced
    to be with each other,
From mother and father,
    to sister and brother.

The youngest son, Tiny Tim,
    hobbled in on his crutch.
He was sickly and weak, but good as
    gold and beloved much.
"Oh, spirit," asked Scrooge,
    "will poor Tiny Tim live?"
A grim answer was all
    that the Spirit could give.

"In shadows, a vacant seat
   and lonely crutch see I.
If his future is unaltered,
   the child will die—
But his death would decrease
   the surplus population."
Scrooge's head hung at hearing
   his own proclamation.

They next watched at nephew
  Fred's big Christmas party,
Where the guests were all bright,
  their laughs rich and hearty.
Scrooge found himself happily
  joining with the merry folk,
As they played their fun games
  and told many a joke.

Such scenes of Christmas cheer
   were repeated by the ghost,
The lessons of charity and mercy
   being foremost.
Rays of love began to melt
   old Scrooge's frosty heart,
And he then knew that Christmas
   had more to impart.

Christmas is a blessing,
   a day of giving and sharing,
The chance to be near family,
   practice kindness and caring.
When the whole wintry world
   seems so bleak and full of strife,
Christmastime brings love, joy,
   and laughter to life.

The Ghost of Christmas Present
had grown clearly older,
But he taught Scrooge these precepts
—over and over.
At the stroke of midnight
on that Christmas Day,
The spirit, like the sunset,
then faded away.

Through the mist came a gloomy,
black-hooded phantom,
The last specter: The Ghost
of Christmas Yet to Come.
Quivered Scrooge, "Your purpose
is to do good for me;
With a thankful heart, I'll heed.
Please show what may be."

While the Present had been
  so pleasant and cheery,
The Future seeped in
  all shrouded and dreary.
On a corner in the busiest
  part of the city
A man's death was heralded
  with no show of pity.

Some friendless soul
  had passed on in the night,
And no friends or mourners
  could be found in sight.
His death was occasion
  for benefit and plunder;
Thieves had even torn his
  bed curtains asunder.

Aghast, Scrooge pleaded,
  "Is there no tenderness?
In death there should be love
  and grief to express!"
To the home of the Cratchits then
  Scrooge went once more,
But no joy, only grief, lay at
  their humble door.

The family wept for the passing
  of poor Tiny Tim,
And Scrooge found himself silently
  weeping with them.
"Who," he then asked, though the
  answer he feared,
"Was the cursed man whose death
  was so mocked and so jeered?"

Scrooge was conveyed next
to an old, forlorn church
Surrounded by graves;
    his heart gave a lurch.
"Are these all the shadows
    of what Will or May be?
Surely futures can change. Say it's
    true, even for me."

With one silent motion replied the
  hooded ghost.
"Oh, spirit!" trembled Scrooge,
  "I do fear you the most.
Pray tell that a man
  can for ill deeds atone!"
With horror Scrooge read
  his own name on the tombstone.

EBENEZER
SCROOGE

With a start, Scrooge was back in
    his bed, now awake.
With exuberance, he gave his
    bed curtains a shake.
He praised Heaven and Christmastime
    while down on his knees;
Swore to honor the season
    and others to please.

He laughed and then danced,
  his heart filled with joy.
He felt just as giddy
  as a merry schoolboy!
Throwing open his window,
  he called to a young lad,
And sent him to fetch
  the grandest turkey to be had!

To Bob Cratchit's he sent
the big turkey with glee
And vowed to raise good Bob's
deficient salary.
Dear Scrooge was far better
than his promised word,
As good a friend, man, or master
in all of the world.

Of him it was said
   that he kept Christmas well,
Past, Present, and Future
   did in his heart dwell.
"God bless us, every one," said
   Tiny Tim in fading light.
A happy Christmas to all,
   and to all a good night.

Scrooge's Night Before Christmas
First Edition
20 19 18 17 16   5 4 3 2 1

Text © 2016 Julie Petersen
Illustrations © 2016 Gibbs Smith

Published by
Gibbs Smith
P.O. Box 667
Layton, Utah 84041

1.800.835.4993 orders
www.gibbs-smith.com

Designed and illustrated by Sheryl Dickert
Printed and bound in China

Gibbs Smith books are printed on either recycled,
100% post-consumer waste, FSC-certified papers
or on paper produced from sustainable PEFC-
certified forest/controlled wood source. Learn
more at www.pefc.org.

Library of Congress Control
    Number: 2016933254
ISBN 978-1-4236-4489-7